© 1994, Editorial LIBSA
Published by GRANGE BOOKS,
an imprint of Grange Books plc
The Grange, Grange Yard
London SE1 3AG

Published 1994

Illustrated by: JULIAN JORDAN and EVA LOPEZ

Text by: María de Calonje
Translated by: Carmen Healy
Phototypesetting by: Versal Composición, S.L.
Printed by: Gráficas Reunidas, S.A.

ISBN: 1-85627-603-1 Legal Dep.: M 19.105 - 1994

The Little Mermaid

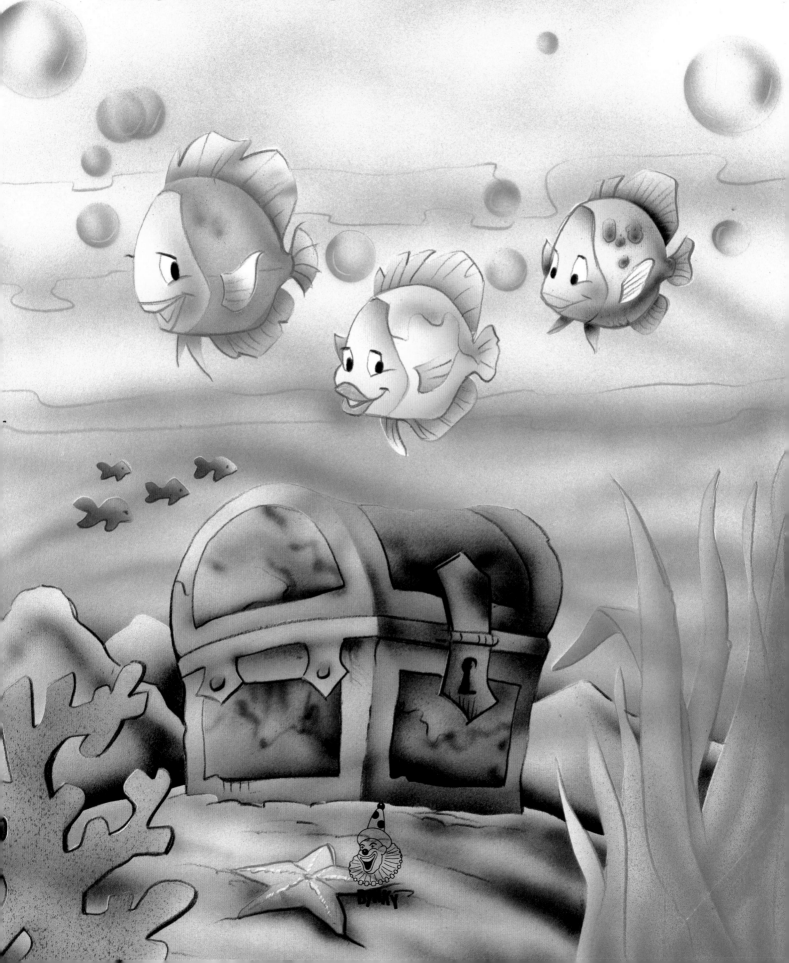

Far out in the ocean, beneath the blue, transparent water, deep down at the very bottom, live the sea people.

In that underwater world, among marvellous plants and colourful fish, is the palace of the Sea King.

The widowed king had six lovely daughters and of these princesses, the youngest was the prettiest of all.

Her skin was very soft and her eyes very blue; but she didn't have feet. Just like her sisters and all the sea people, her body ended in a fish tail. She was a mermaid.

This little mermaid loved to hear stories of the world of men and continuously asked her grandmother to tell her about ships, human beings and animals. These things she knew only from the small objects found in shipwrecks that she carefully saved in her room.

"When you reach fifteen, I will give you permission to go to the surface of the sea. You can sit in the moonlight on the shore, watch the great ships and see the forest and the cities," their grandmother told them one day.

The following year, the eldest of the daughters reached fifteen. Since there was a difference of a year between each one of them, the youngest would have to wait five more years to leave the bottom of the sea. Each of them promised to tell in complete detail everything they saw in the outside world.

At last the day arrived when the eldest of the princesses went to the surface. When she returned, she had a thousand things to tell.

"Oh! How delightful it is to see the big city while basking in the moonlight on a lovely beach. The lights shine like hundreds of stars. The music, the sound of the church bells, the noise of the carriages, people walking the streets of the harbour. It's all marvellous".

Our little mermaid was happy listening to her sister.

The following year, the second sister received permission to surface and told her sisters the wonders of that magnificent sight.

So the princesses each swam up to the surface until it was the youngest mermaid's turn.

When her head first rose above the sea the sun was setting. The sky and the clouds were a brilliant purple. The air was sweet and fresh and the sea was calm. Close to the little mermaid was a lovely three masted ship with the sails unfurled. The sailors were sitting on deck, singing and admiring, as she was, the magnificent sunset.

The little mermaid approached the ship to have a better look at what was happening. When the waves lifted her up, she saw many magnificently dressed men. The most handsome of them all was a young prince whose birthday was on that day. That was the reason for the festivities on the ship.

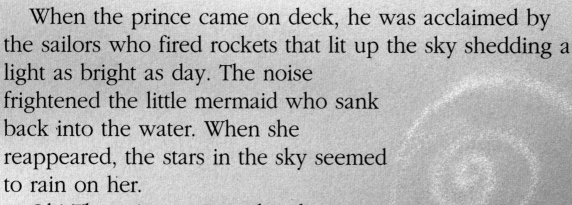

When the prince came on deck, he was acclaimed by the sailors who fired rockets that lit up the sky shedding a light as bright as day. The noise frightened the little mermaid who sank back into the water. When she reappeared, the stars in the sky seemed to rain on her.

Oh! The prince was so handsome. He shook everyone's hand. He spoke and smiled to everyone while the music sent its harmonious sound into the night.

When the little mermaid was about to return to the deep sea, it began to get rough. The waves grew and great black storm clouds gathered in the sky. Far off lightning flashed A terrible storm was brewing.

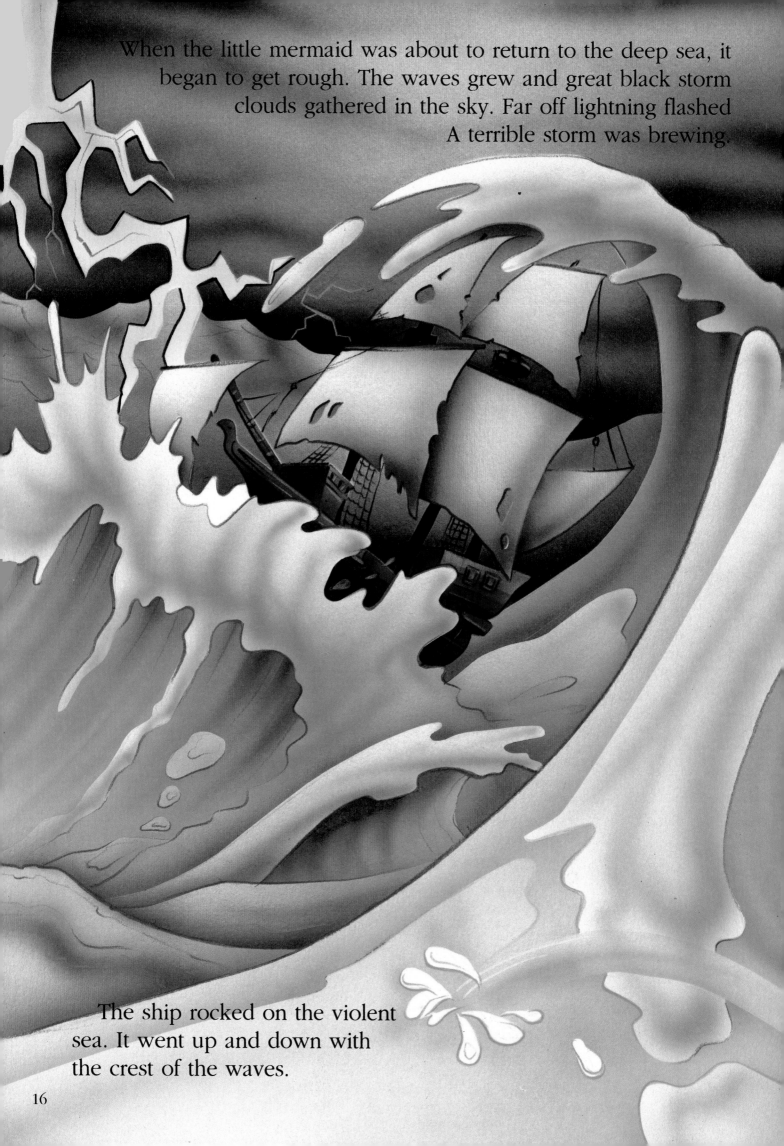

The ship rocked on the violent sea. It went up and down with the crest of the waves.

The lights went on again on the ship, and the sailors hurriedly took in the sails. The little mermaid was at first happy to see such an unexpected sight, but she understood the danger as the ship shook violently. It's timbers began to creak, the largest mast snapped like a twig, then the ship tilted to one side and water began to enter the hold. Even the little mermaid had to be careful not to get hit by the enormous pieces of wood that floated around her.

It was all very dark, and she could hardly see anything.
Only when the lightning illuminated the sky could she make
out the sailors clinging to driftwood to save themselves. She
looked for the prince and saw him sinking into the deep sea.
Joyfully she thought he was going down to her domain but
suddenly she remembered that men cannot live under the sea
and therefore he would drown.

"The prince can't die, he must not die,"
thought the little mermaid.

She swam rapidly and reached him just
when his strength began to leave him and
he was closing his eyes about to drown.
She grasped him with all her might, held
his head above the water and waited for
the terrible storm to pass.

The next morning the calm had returned, but there was nothing left of the ship. The prince was still unconscious. The little mermaid kissed his forehead and fervently wished he would live.

She then saw a beach and headed there so that the prince could recover in a safe place. She reached it with great effort. She went to hide behind some rocks and waited for someone to come.

When someone arrived and found the prince and he had regained consciousness, she sadly sank into the sea and returned to her father's house.

When her sisters asked her what she had seen up at the surface she said nothing about the prince.

More than once, at dusk or at dawn, she would return to the place where she had left the prince, but she didn't see him. Her fondness for humans grew from day to day. Their world seemed more attractive than her own. Each time she was more sure of her love for the prince. She no longer liked living in the sea.

One day she couldn't control herself anymore and she told her grandmother.

"Dear child," replied her grandmother, "just as men cannot live in the water, we cannot live on land."

"Isn't there any way that I can become a human being?" asked the little mermaid.

"Just one, but it is almost impossible. A man must fall in love with you and his every thought must be of you. Then, bound to you with all his heart and soul, he must promise you everlasting faithfulness, and when his soul enters your body, you can become a human being."

"But," continued her grandmother, "such a thing could never happen. Your fish tail, which is considered beautiful here in the sea, seems loathsome to those on land. To be lovely, they believe it is necessary to have those two columns they call legs."

The little mermaid sighed sadly looking at her fish tail.

"Cheer up," said her grandmother, "have fun and be happy enjoying life. Remember that we have three hundred years of existence and that men live much less. Also remember that tonight, your father the king is giving a grand ball in the palace."

No one who lives on land could imagine such magnificence. The ceiling and the walls of the grand ballroom were made of glass. Thousands of enormous pink, blue and green snails were lined up on each side illuminating the room with a blue light that, through the transparent walls, also lit up the sea. In the middle of the ballroom, mermaids and tritons danced to the sound of their delightful songs. The little mermaid was the best singer and they applauded her so much that, for an instant, she forgot the wonders of land. But soon she returned to her grief, remembering the prince and her love for him.

"I'm going to do everything possible to get him to love me too," the young mermaid said to herself. "While the others are enjoying themselves at the ball, I'm going to look for the sea witch. Perhaps she can advise and help me."

The little mermaid headed for the Darksea abyss, where the witch lived. It was a sinister place where she had never been. As she got nearer there were fewer and fewer plants until only rocks and sand remained. Feeling awfully frightened, she thought of returning, but she was caught in the terrible whirlpools that would drag her to the witch's domain.

Suddenly the whirlpools stopped, but the terrible sight that lay before her eyes seized her with fear. The evil inhabitants of those depths had imprisoned the carcasses of land animals, the treasure chests from shipwrecks and many horrible things. Terrifying sea snakes looked at her with flashing eyes that were full of menace.

She was in front of the witch's cave. Surrounded by her frightening snakes, the witch was feeding an enormous and revolting toad from her hand.

"I know what you want," she exclaimed at the sight of the little mermaid. "Your wishes are ridiculous, but I will help you because I know it will bring you disgrace. You want to get rid of your fish tail and replace it with those columns that humans walk with, so that the prince falls in love and marries you."

Finishing with these words, she let out such a terrifying laugh that the toad fell from her hands.

"Good, you did well to come today. Tomorrow at dawn would have been too late and you would have had to wait a whole year. I am going to prepare a potion that you will carry to shore before the day breaks. When you arrive, sit on the coast and drink it. At once your tail will writhe and divide in two, forming what humans call two pretty legs. But I warn you that this will hurt as if you were cut by a sharp sword. All will admire the grace of your walk and no ballerina in the whole kingdom will compare to you."

"Bear in mind," she continued, "that once you become human, you cannot return to being a mermaid again. You will never see your father or sisters again. You can never go back to the bottom of the sea."

"I accept all the conditions," the princess said pale as a ghost.

"In that case, you should pay me the price I ask."

"Tell me what you want," murmured the scared mermaid.

"I want your voice," said the witch. "Your voice is the loveliest under the sea, you could charm your prince with it, but that's precisely what I want, I want your voice."

"But if you take my voice, what do I have left?"

"Your charming figure," replied the witch. "Your light and graceful walk. That will be enough to win the heart of your prince."

"So be it," whispered the little mermaid.

Immediately the witch began to prepare the magic potion. While she did so, she laughed sarcastically. When she was nearly finished, she asked the little mermaid to sing. So, little by little, while the potion brewed, the witch was taking her voice. When she was completely mute, she was given a flask with the elixir.

The princess took it and nodded her head. She could no longer speak.

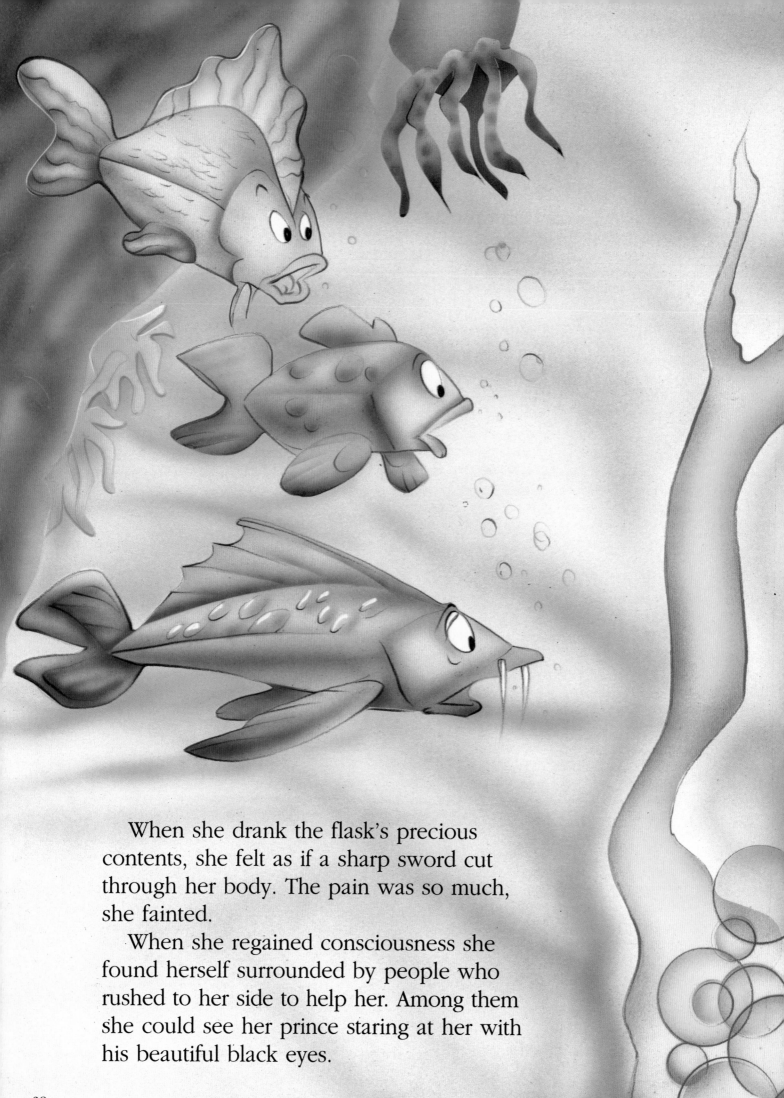

When she drank the flask's precious
contents, she felt as if a sharp sword cut
through her body. The pain was so much,
she fainted.

When she regained consciousness she
found herself surrounded by people who
rushed to her side to help her. Among them
she could see her prince staring at her with
his beautiful black eyes.

The prince took her in his arms and carried her to his palace so that the court doctors could care for her. The little mermaid looked at him delightedly and the prince felt his heart leap.

They settled her in one of the most beautiful rooms of the palace so she could rest. Every day, in the morning and in the afternoon, the prince visited her. They spent long hours together, looking at each other, fascinated.

One morning, the prince seemed different.

"I don't know if it was a dream," he said, "but last night I think I remembered who you are. You saved my life when my ship sank. I don't know how, but you did it. I could never forget your eyes. I fell in love with them at once."

"Tell me it wasn't a dream," continued the young prince gently holding her hands.

The little mermaid softly nodded her head.

The prince then said, "Will you be my wife?"

All of a sudden the miracle occurred! She recovered her lovely voice! 'Yes," she answered.

They lived happily ever after

44